Not My Mom Anymore
by P G Seshagopal

Table of Contents

This short story is entirely a work of fiction and meant solely for the purpose of entertainment. All characters, names of characters, places, buildings, events, and incidents portrayed in it are the work of the author's imagination and are purely fictitious. Any resemblance/similarities to actual persons, living or dead, events or localities is entirely coincidental and not intentional. The author shall not be responsible or liable in any manner whatsoever for the same. This novel work is not meant to defame/denigrate/hurt sentiments of any person, community, institution, or any class of person(s), gender, caste, or religion in any manner.

Chapter – 1: Ears Ringing

Just another happy day. From the morning, getting praises from everyone near me, including my never-smile class teacher.

Cracked third rank in the class, won speech and writing competition for children below seven years. A dream day, not because of the thundering claps from my classmates and teachers, because of the extreme happiness of the person most special to me. Received plenty of kisses and hugs.

Of course, nothing new about my mom hugging and kissing me. Almost every day starts like that for me. Yet, when I achieve something, all I want is her smile and praise. Everything in the world comes second to that feeling of warm hugs and soft kisses on the cheek.

After getting a surprise visit from our Headmaster after lunch hours, eagerly waiting for the end of hours school bell to ring. Picturing the image of me jumping into mom's arms with a big smile.

Each and every bit of the praise goes to mom. She taught me everything. The school teachers explain, but they are little strict, and I am not entirely comfortable in asking them doubts. Dad says, in the class of forty students, it is difficult to clear everyone's doubt. Maybe he is right.

Don't have any problem in asking doubts to mom. She will always reply politely and makes me understand. Even learning is fun with her, unlike at school. She studies all my subjects, knows every lesson in my book and way too smarter. Very rarely she makes mistakes in studies. It gives me immense pleasure to point out her mistake.

Till date, don't remember a single day that had gone by without warm hugs and soft kisses. Every day wakes up watching her charming face and goes to sleep looking at her smile.

I don't mind losing to her, and she doesn't mind losing to me. Not the same when I play along with friends.

She had never yelled at me like some of these harsh teachers. Never beat me. Dad does sometimes scream when I try to play with him, especially when he is working on his stupid laptop.

When mom cooks, I will always sit next to her on a chair and keep watching what she is doing. Though, have no idea of what's going on, like the final result of tasty food.

Grandma and Grandpa occasionally visit us. Whenever they come, they will have a gift for me. Only after a nod from mom, will accept that. Till date, had never asked for any toy or gift. Whatever mom gets me, will play with it. More than toys, puzzles, chess, and video games, love playing with her. Though I have friends to play with, my biggest fun is playing with her.

Never ate the food of my own hands. Dad is forcing me nowadays; I still eat from my mother's hand. It adds an extra taste. I kind of feel dad is one of the villains for me. He always tries to do something like this that makes me feel sad.

The main villain is my aunt, Suji. Suji equals to "*Torture*" Only for the past three months she is staying with us in the name of studying college. One hundred percent sure, she is not at all going to college. She is cheating everyone in the family. She wears weird dresses, weird colours, and nothing like mom.

Suji aunty keeps on mocking me. Pinches me for nothing. Always falsely claims she is more beautiful than my mom. Suji aunty is the ugliest, whew... you will sure throw up if you watch her ugly face for five minutes. Shows her pale white skin as her proof, a result of multiple coating of painting done by her in the name of makeup. Suji aunty is an evil demon that comes on comics and tortures little kids for fun. She is the worst of worst.

Even her way of expressing love brings me pain. She pinches hard, drags my cheeks and kisses hard, so severely, usually I wash my face after that kiss. Always wonder, she can't be mom's younger sister? I am confident that she is adopted. One day will confirm that with the Grandparents.

Running deep into the thoughts of my aunt, the school bell for the end of hours shook me. Took the bag immediately and jumped out of my place. Ran as fast as I can towards the gate to cuddle into mom's arms.

Something is not usual. Mom is talking with the headmaster. Reduced the speed and slowly walked towards them.

The headmaster nodded his head in agreement and told, *"You can join from Monday, Mrs Akash."* Why HM said dad's name? What are they talking about? Where dad is going to join? The HM realised my presence, patted on my shoulder, smiled, and left.

Waited for him to take a few steps away from me. Laughed out loud and jumped into my mother's arm. Hugged her tightly and said, 'You know, everyone praised me today. Even the HM came to our class and celebrated with us. Everyone loves me.'

Mom kissed on the cheek and smiled, 'Of course! You are a superstar! Knew my sweetheart will win and everyone will admire.'

More laughter and hugging. As usual, grabbed my mom's hand and juggled our way back to the home.

Before opening the door, mom bent down towards me and in excitement, 'One pleasant surprise for you. From next week

Monday, I am going to come with you to the school and teach little kids of KG classes. We can have lunch together and come back home together.'

Initially, I smiled, merely looking at her excitement. Slowly felt something was not right. She is going to teach kids like me? Is she going to be a teacher at my school? Oh my God! No, she can't become that person with a serious face, yells at kids for little mistakes and strict on everything. No, definitely she meant something else.

My face slowly turning from extreme happiness to complete sadness. Mom understood my expression and her smile also reduced gradually. Felt one question will make everything clear. 'Are you going to be a teacher?' in a doubtful tone asked her, hoping and praying for the answer to be "*No*" Mom smiled mildly, 'Yes. I will teach KG classes, like Dhivya madam.'

Dhivya madam was one of my favourite teachers, and I like her very much. But, that's not the answer I wanted to hear. It is a complete shock. My mom is going to be a teacher? I can hear my teacher yelling at me for talking with my bench-mate. Their strict rules, making me stand up on the bench for my handwriting.

No, my mom can't be like that. Suddenly all I can hear is a bell ringing. It's ringing louder and louder on my ears. Mom appeared worried, and she is saying something to me. I couldn't hear a single word. It kept on ringing.

Will my mom have time for me? Will she talk the same way as before? Do I have the right to say "*My Mom?*" I looked clueless and blinked my eyes continuously. So many questions and my fears are doubling each passing second.

Desperately wanted to go into the bedroom and cuddle the pillow tightly. Quickly got into the house, even though I can see mom's worried look. Stood halfway in the middle of the hall and turned towards mom.

With a sad face, asking questions through expressions, looking at mom, why you did this to me, mom? What wrong had I done? Why this punishment? Will you ever be my mom again? I can see the sadness on mom's face. Without saying a word rushed into the room.

Chapter – 2: Lost Everything

Tears were pouring out like a flood. Irrespective of how hard I try, can't stop my tears. Screamed in pain. It's unbearable.

Had locked the door and didn't respond to mom when she knocked the door. Though it is said to be my room, it was never. It's mine and mom's room. Dad rarely comes here. Everything in the room reminds me of my mom.

Can hear the voice of dad and the knock on the door. Didn't reply to him either. He only makes things even worse by his advice and philosophies that I couldn't understand.

I had to do something soon. Mom says to figure out the core of any problem, ask questions from different angles. Never understood what exactly she meant. But, decided to give a try as every word of her means so much to me.

Threw the pillow in anger and got down from the bed. Walked across the room and stood at an angle. Closed my eyes and deep into thinking about the problem.

Let's try something different. *"What mistakes I recently commit?" Made fun of dad.* Did mom got angry for that and punishing me like this?

Though mom does always take my side, she always has a high place in her heart for dad. Sometimes have a curious feeling to know who is more important to her. She almost worships him and always suggest to consider dad above teachers and God.

He can't be greater than God? He is less smart than mom, at times, yells, angry looks, forget things, and cooks terribly. He can't survive a day without mom. How can someone like him be more significant than God?

Not able to figure this part out. Let's say mom is angry with me because of teasing dad, all I have to do is ask sorry. Though dad is a villain type, a sorry is all he expects in return. The next minute, he will forget everything and throws me up in the air and catch.

A pleasant smile came on my face at last. The happiness grew. Mom is right again. Thinking from a different angle does work. Ok, let's try various other angles.

Walked across at an angle and reached near the bed. Again, tried the same approach, but can't think beyond dad. Opened my eyes and turned around the room. Something is not right in this place.

Went near the door and repeated the process. *Forgot to put empty milk cup in the sink.* Yes, that's a good enough reason.

After trying from different angles, plenty of ideas came in mind. Figured out a possible solution for each one of them with perfectly scripted apologies. Writing practice given by mom helped.

Confidence is at sky level and hundred percent sure of convincing mom. Opened the door and walked without making any noise like a kitten.

Dad sitting on the sofa at the hall, working on his laptop, saw me in extreme anger and yelled, 'What is this new habit of locking the door? From where you...'

Completely shuddered, froze for a second. The moment mom heard this, she came running from the kitchen and in a loud pitch, 'Akash!'

Dad controlled his anger and stopped the outburst. Mom indicated some signal. Both mom and dad exchanged signals as usual, which only they can understand.

Dad's face changed barely in ten seconds. That's the magic of mom. 'Shall we have dinner, sweetheart?' Mom said politely.

Wanted to reply *"Only from your hands."* But, the fear of dad's anger made me nod a *"Yes"* immediately.

We sat in our usual positions around the dining table. Dad, at the centre on the chair, mom next to him and me on top of the table, chewing tasty food from mom's hand.

We had finished dinner, and mom is going to finish. Usually, mom will eat last, and I will patiently wait sitting next to her. Dad sometimes will sit and serve mom, sometimes won't.

I hesitantly asked, 'Mom, are you angry on me?' Mom immediately swallowed the half-chewed food in her mouth and replied, 'No, my darling. I will never be angry with you. Had I ever been angry?'

In utter disappointment, 'Then, why are you becoming a teacher?' Mom gave her usual delightful smile, 'Because, after you go to school, I am getting bored sitting alone at home. No one is here to chat or play with me. To pass my time, doing what I like, a teaching job.'

In frustration, kicked the chair next to me, 'If you are bored, go to dad's office or any other office or ask me to stay at home itself, don't become a teacher.'

Her smile making me weak. But her expression didn't change a bit, 'I had to do what I like, right? Spending time with sweet, cute, and smart kids like you bring me plenty of happiness. If I don't do something that makes me happy, it wouldn't be correct.'

My face dropped. Looked down at the floor for a while. Mom finished dinner, washed her hands, plates, and came back to the hall, where I was sitting on the one corner of the sofa. Dad sat on the other end.

Mom touched my face and rolled her fingers as soft as a feather. I looked up and asked my first question, 'Are you doing this because I mocked dad? I will seek plea sorry and convince him now itself. Will accept any other punishment.'

Dad suddenly turned towards me in complete shock and looked at me curiously. Mom sat on the sofa and embraced me. 'Sweetheart, I am not angry on you or doing this because of anything else. You are the greatest, sweet, and beautiful boy. You always listen to me and had never done anything wrong.

I always wanted to become a teacher. It's my dream. Why are you feeling sad about this? There is nothing to worry. Mom will always be there for you.'

I didn't hear a single word from mom. Kept on asking all the questions that I thought of from various angles in my room. Mom kept on denying everything and trying to console me.

After few questions, dad slowly started to smile and then, laughed out loud like a killer villain. Mom signalled him to keep quiet. Finally, I lost my patience, broke out crying and screaming.

Mom pulling me, trying to cuddle and stop me from crying. I tried to move away forcefully. 'You will never be the same again. You will not be... my mom anymore. You will become like those cruel, evil, harsh, and strict teachers. You won't care about me anymore. You won't be mine anymore.'

Mom in her same sweet voice, 'I will always be your mom. Nothing will change. You are my sweet son. I... I will be like Dhivya mam, soft and caring. I will always love you and take care of you.'

I went on to my knees and in a husky voice, 'Please mom! Don't become a teacher. Be only my mom.'

Mom combed my hair by her fingers, 'Nothing will change between us. You and I will play and enjoy every day as we are doing now. In fact, more teachers will become your friends, and more kids like you will love me.'

That's it. I had enough. Forcefully pushed her hands and got up in full anger. 'Don't want any teacher as my friend and don't want any other kid to love you. Want only you.'

Mom is almost going to cry as she couldn't bear seeing me crying. She was about to say something, dad placed his hands her shoulder and politely, 'Hema?'

Mom looked at him, tears going to burst out from her eyes. Again, they signalled, and mom quietly turned towards dad.

That was the final unkindest blow for me. This can't be my mom. Shook my head, crying, slowly walked backwards, and yelled, 'You are not my mom anymore!' Then, in a depressed, sad tone, 'Not my mom anymore!'

Turned around and about to ran towards my room, while the worst person in the world knocked on the door and from behind the door, devil Suji aunty shouted, 'My chubby darling! Chubby.... chubby... Wait for me, don't go to sleep!'

Definitely didn't want to hear that evil demon's voice now. Ran towards the room, while my mom in a loud tone, 'Krish... Krish! Stop...' Kept on calling me to stop. I don't want to look at her. Rushed into the room and immediately locked the door.

Jumped on the bed and tightly hugged the pillow. Couldn't stop the tears and kept on shouting, "*Why you did this to me? Why?*"

I can't help the feeling of losing everything ever meant to me. Had lost my mom. She is never coming back.

Chapter – 3: My Precious

"Change is the only permanent thing in life!" A quote that I firmly believe. Life was easy when we were young. As we grew up, it does get harder.

My parents, even today keeps on bragging about little cute things I did as a child. All my relatives considered me as the naughtiest child ever born in our family.

They are right of course. Even in my college days, doing pranks, teasing my friends comes naturally for me. Dad deserves a lot of credit for how I turned up. He taught me to be fearless, confident, and enjoy every single moment of my life.

Being talk active for the most part of the childhood, have the luxury of so many friends. Studying is a process of learning for me, from the day I can remember. Likes to practically implement the theories.

A carefree, joyous, and pleasant life where money, time, place, or anything had no significance. Like everybody, who was born on the early nineties, I too studied engineering, as it almost became a mandate for middle-class people. My passion was always to become a teacher who takes classes for young little kids. It remained a dream.

While studying last year at college, on the verge of becoming a horrible engineering graduate, dad's heart attack trembled our entire family. Retiring from his government job, dad's only wish was to arrange the marriage for me to a dependable person using his PF money.

Many days fought with my parents, trying to convince them that I can earn and help my younger sister, Sujitha's education.

Always lost the battle. On the frag end of the arguments, my parents and relatives successfully persuaded me for marriage.

Akash came with his mom and relatives for a tradition of groom visiting bride before engagement. After our first meeting itself, felt that there was nothing common in between us and I am going to live my rest of the life unhappily.

He is not talk-active, definitely not funny, grim looks, moody, and dull. My exact opposite. I was very sure that I am not ready for the responsibilities of marriage. Yet, agreed for the wedding only for dad. A traditional arranged marriage.

Dad and mom always wanted and gave me only the best. My trust started to pay off soon after the marriage. Admired Akash's silence, gritty looks, he is handsome and influenced me by his sheer charm. He never raised a voice or seriously argued for anything. Always with a mild smile. He tolerated by over-talking, worse cooking, pranks, and end of the day, greets with a soft little peck on my cheek.

Felt blessed to have such a husband, especially after having discussions with my close friends about their marriage life. He is the best thing that happened in my life. Caring and loving, handsome young man.

I didn't want to go for the job and rejected offer letter, only because of Akash's support. Additional income could have helped us for sure. Just for my happiness, he let me choose and didn't speak against my will, not even a single word.

This didn't stop him from taking responsibility for my family. He paid for dad's expensive medical treatment and Suji's tuition fees. He just took it as his duty and never made any fuss about it. Everyone in my family holds Akash every high in their hearts and respect him deeply. Who wouldn't?

I became more mature. Every day is a learning curve for me and learnt so much from my mother-in-law. Gifted in that department too. The naughtiness and mischiefs are only available for my one and only, Akash. He liked me more for that.

Though I am not the blushing type, I will do it then and there, because he likes it. Seeing him happy makes me happier.

After six months of a perfect marriage, something very new happened in our life. The arrival of a new member. Still remember the first time when I felt a life within me, growing ever so slowly. One of the most important and joyous moments of my life, conveying my pregnancy to Akash and admiring his reaction.

Felt my life became whole, because of this new life growing inside me. From a complete careless girl, became an extremely precautious woman. Cautious of food, temperature, climate, floor, furniture... woo...f! The list goes on. Sometimes will have panic attacks too. Akash endured it all with the same mild, pretty smile.

The happiest day of my life till date, to hold Krish on my hands for the very first time. Couldn't remember the pain I underwent during delivery. Barely 3 kilograms, little eyes like me, cutest baby ever born. I believe every mother feels the same way. The day my Precious arrived in this world is the most special day for me.

Blessed to have the cutest child in the world. Krish became my centre of attention, and my highest priority is to take care of him.

Very rarely I gave attention to Akash. Till date, he hasn't shown or complained a word about it. He will be awake in the midnight when I try to make Krish sleep. Though Akash is little afraid on holding him for the first three months, as Krish's neck was not stiff, Akash slowly got the confidence and spent more time holding him.

My heartbeat raises to sky-high whenever Akash throws Krish up in the air and catches him. Krish will smile big and sometimes laughs out loud. Tried to tell Akash not to do that indirectly, but mixed emotions made me drop the idea from further proceeding.

A day starts thinking of my dear son and ends the same way. Always felt terrible whenever Krish cries. He very rarely cries, mostly when he is hungry.

Whenever Krish gets sick or cry, always felt that I am the worst mother in the world. How irresponsible and careless am I? Kept on blaming myself for at least a couple of days, and become more cautious. Akash has to go through a lot on those days.

Krish is the most obedient child I have ever seen.

One day, when Akash was searching for a document, shouting, and calling for me, made Krish sit and told him not to move an inch. With those small eyes, he looked at me sadly, making me feel worse. Forced a horse toy on his hands and ran towards Akash.

After two hours, when I came back to the room, Krish was sitting in the same position eagerly waiting to see my face, raised his arms seeking to lift him with a big smile. How many times he might have expected my face? Did he ever take-off his eyes away from the door? How patient is he?

Had any energetic and active child sat on the same position for two hours before? I don't think so. My words mean a lot to him. He never says "*no*" to me. If I say don't do to a thing, he will never do that.

He rarely leaves my side. Even in the kitchen, placed a chair for him to sit a little away from the stove. He will there for hours, simply looking at me, waving his hands and legs; occasionally smiles when I look towards him.

Prepared for his naughtiness, considering my childhood memories. Zero, zilch, nothing of that. Mother-in-law says Akash was like that, silent, calm and always listening to elders.

Honestly, I am disappointed. Krish is my boy. He must do some mischiefs. Don't want another xerox copy of Akash. So, made Krish talk more and he will talk... talk... and never stops. He plays with full energy and gives it a cent percent every time. I might get tired, Akash might get tired, he never does. Concluded he is as expected a mixture of us both.

Suji and my parents shifted to a house in the same town. Akash wanted them to stay in the same house, but my dad's pride didn't allow that. Suji will come on weekends and play with Krish.

Krish does not likes Suji getting close to me. He forcefully pushes her away and gives angry looks when Suji claims *"her sister first and mom next."* Krish will give a loud *"No"* and says, *"Only my mom!"*

He got that possessiveness from me. My precious, mine only. Though on necessity must leave Krish with grandparents sometimes, still can't tolerate Krish giving more importance to them than me. They can be second or third choice... but not the first preference.

The warm hugs, sweet smiles, polite enquires, little pecks on the cheek, a pleasure only a mother can understand. Krish is so special and can keep on thinking about his cute acts all my day.

Each moment, when I think about him, brings a smile on my face.

Chapter – 4: Unbearable

Krish grew up very fast. The death of my mother-in-law did put all in grievances for a long time. I missed her the most or probably everyone who knew her felt that way.

Both Akash and me showered love and so much love on Krish. Nobody till now needed to be strict as Krish is too sweet to do any mischiefs. We both discussed at some point one of us must become strict on him.

Was hoping that day would never occur. But it was inevitable. Krish cried a lot after getting a syringe in the form of vaccination. The next vaccination came after a period of two months, didn't go well with him.

At the nearby school, where they inject, Krish went into a zone of a tantrum. He sat down on the floor, screamed, and begged not to inject. While almost everyone at the school advised me to carry on, I couldn't. His tears made me weaker. All the little kids cried, but their parents forcefully took them.

One or two kids who went extreme left with their parents. One of the nurses understood my difficulty and suggested me to come on any of the remaining three days of the campaign.

At home, Akash showed his displeasure for not injecting Krish. This is a very serious and critical vaccination that we shouldn't ignore. My brain can understand, but my heart couldn't. Just, don't have the heart to see Krish cry, scream, and beg. He is the sweetest and coolest child one could ever have and hadn't objected anything till date.

How can I force such a nice little kid? That's not possible for me to do. Went as far as possible, defending Krish. Even told

Akash few examples of old people who are naturally immune, never took these vaccinations and lived for hundred years.

I think that idiotic logic made Akash take a firm decision. He concluded that he will be the stricter parent and he is not going to risk his son's life because he cries. First time I heard Akash speaking in a deafening tone.

Next day, when Akash asked Krish to come, he understood for what his dad is forcing him. Krish tried to hide behind me and sorted my help to convince his dad.

Akash face turned slowly from anger to cruel. He yelled thunderously, 'Stop crying!' Even I shook and froze for a second. Poor little Krish stopped crying and opened his little eyes fully in complete shock and fear.

Akash forcefully grabbed Krish's hand and dragged him. Without a word, Krish went behind him. Neither of them turned back. The husband who has never even raised his voice against me yelled at such a high pitch that the ceiling might have ripped off.

Understood the necessity of Akash's firm and harsh attitude on this. They came back after two hours, and Krish had a sad and grim face. Krish ran towards me and hugged tightly. It seems he didn't cry on injection as well.

My good-looking husband kept Krish intact. The next time Akash has to show his other face was on Krish's first day at school. My sweetheart calmly got ready for the school at home. Only when we are going to leave, he began to cry.

One angry, furious face and one shrill yell, that's all it took to keep Krish silent. Without a word, Krish sadly went and sat inside the classroom and never looked back. Akash is scary when he is angry, and I don't like to see him like that. My hubby will turn from erupting volcano to chill snow in a matter of a second. A rare gift and quality that he possesses.

From that day, Krish's school time was the most challenging period. Tried different things like going to the gym, hanging out with neighbouring moms, gossip groups and so on. Nothing worked out. Day by day was getting restless and bored during that time.

Akash frequently asked about my comfort at home, when nobody was there. I convinced him that I am doing perfectly fine. Slowly, during lunchtime call with Akash, expressed by feeling.

After a year, Akash suggested me to take a job that is somehow related to teaching. Initially was utterly against it, reasoning him couldn't be able to take care and manage him and Krish. My darling tried to persuade me many times through various theories and examples. He always assures his full support and everything will turn out amazing.

This year beginning was a pleasant surprise for me as Suji decided to stay at our home as it is nearer to her college. The main reason is to reduce her travel time.

Suji's arrival didn't help me much either. She too wasn't available at that time and once again became alone. The boredom reached its peak. Finally, decided to do what I always dreamt.

Everyone was supportive, and it was Akash's idea to not tell Krish. He foresaw how Krish will behave on knowing his mom is going to be a teacher.

As he expected, Krish didn't want me to do it. The slow turn before going into his room and sad eyes staring at me asking questions were like thousand swords piercing right through my heart.

Krish had never locked his room door before. Today, he did and didn't respond to my knock on the door or my call. Akash came, and he tried his part too. He consoled me by making me realise Krish acted as expected and only need to be patient for a little while.

Akash's point was mainly about how Krish is not getting exposure to the real world. Krish and I became so close that the existence of one is impossible without the other. Akash always says it is the responsibility of parents to make their child take care of themselves, handle the world, make awareness on right and wrong. Krish is definitely not going to get that exposure as long as I am holding him.

Though I agreed on everything my hubby said, was still unable to bear the pain that caused by my son's expressions and words. Never ever thought he would say that I am no longer his mother. That was the most hurtful minutes.

Have Akash's broad shoulder to rest on and cry. His motivational and polite words do bring calmness and reduce grimness. What about Krish? What he might be doing alone? Couldn't sleep the whole night and Akash was awake for me.

Was hoping for a better Saturday. Krish didn't speak with me at all. He ate only a little food by his own hands. He remained sad, inactive, and worrisome. It's unbearable for me to look my cutest boy like this. Hoping for a quick turnaround real soon.

Chapter – 5: A Different Person

Crying for the whole day didn't help me even a bit. Sunday, back to normal, after mom promised me, everything will be the same. Though, I didn't believe her, one day of not speaking with her was like a lifetime.

Was not able to play and enjoy as before. Kept little distance and reduced hugging. Mom understood me, yet, she held the same smile and tried to show like nothing happened.

Monday morning was just like another day. Mom woke up earlier than usual. Prepared food, got me ready for the school and took care of dad too.

My worries are about how my friends would treat me. Surprisingly they took it much more sportively. They felt it is not a big deal at all.

Unexpectedly, my teachers aren't the same. They came to know that I am the son of their co-staff, Hema. I got additional attention, and they spoke sweet and kind words.

One day, when I was not able to answer one of the teacher's questions, she teased me for my incompetence and mentioned *"Teacher's child is a fool"* The whole class laughed at me, including my friends.

Before today, I am considered one of the smartest students in the class. I can speak and write English far better than many of my classmates, even some of our teachers. Practically no one in the class would dare to challenge in essay or story writing. I help most of the boys in writing their leave letters, composition notes and of course assisted teachers in completing their staff workbook.

Couldn't possibly imagine that they actually called me a fool. Tears were in my eyes, but controlled and sat down facing the ground. The humiliation was beyond explainable.

Had shared everything so far to my mom. Didn't felt to share this, though it is important. Ashamed of not knowing the answer. Spent more time in learning and put extra effort. Mom sat with me and taught me the same way she did before.

The first week went rather smoothly than I hoped for. The weekend was a blast as before. Twice teamed up with mom to tease dad.

As usual, Suji aunty angered me saying that *"She is more beautiful than mom"* don't why I didn't want to argue, quietly ignored her, and decided not to talk at all. Has my mom become second to me? No, that can't be true. I do have a slight hesitancy in claiming *"My mom"* I felt she doesn't want me to consider like that anymore.

Next week Wednesday, after the end of school, couldn't find my mom. Scared a little bit, went towards the staffroom. Mom has never left me stranded before. Irrespective of the situation, she will always be on time. This is the first time.

One of the teachers signalled me to stay out of the room. She came outside in a minute and told me to wait, as staff meeting is going on.

More than half an hour gone by and something was wrong with my stomach. I could feel a weird sensation. Maybe that was what others say, *"they are hungry"* More things happened in the stomach and anger started to creep up. Sat down restlessly looking towards the staffroom.

Mom came out running towards me. Filled with both happiness and anger, kept my face grim and looked away. Mom asked sorry plenty of times. Thought of telling her I am hungry, but was not sure what that feeling is. In a sharp tone replied, 'Let's go home and I want something to eat immediately.'

Mom understood what's happening in my stomach. At the gate, she tried to grab my hand, and I forcefully moved away and didn't saw her face, a way of expressing my anger on her. She still remained close to me walking towards the main road.

Before crossing the road, she again tried to hold my hands, and I did the same. We crossed halfway and stood near the divider on the road. One bus overtook another and came at a stunning speed near the divider. It was like as if it is going to hit me.

Quickly jumped in fear and grabbed my mom's hand tightly. The bus went past us making my school Id card fly in the air and hairstyle changed into a spike. Mom softly combed my hair and corrected. Looked at her and smiled modestly.

That night gave a lot of thought. I can barely keep away from mom. Need her to wake me up, cook food, wash my clothes, tie my shoelace, cross the road, do my homework and so on. Yet, for the next one week, kept my distance and didn't fight with my devil aunt.

Next week, mom ensured I have some snacks to eat during the staff meeting. Since the taste of the snack was terrific, didn't complain much. Mom had a big notebook on her hand called notes of the lesson. I think it's somewhat like homework for teachers. Because of working on that notebook, she couldn't help me on the first day.

She told the same reason on the second day too. My homework was a simple three-digit multiplication and division, can do it of my own. But, became restless and can't help the feeling that she is avoiding me purposefully and something is more important to her than me. Bugged her twice or thrice and dad gave anger looks and yelled to solve these simple problems by myself. He could never understand my pain and suffering. Heartless human!

Everyday morning Idli and Coconut chutney became standard. Though it was tasty, slowly getting bored of the same dish daily. It was not like this before when mom was only my mom and not a teacher. Each day will have different food, amazingly yummy.

A couple of days mom woke up late, and we rushed to get ready and ran to school.

Today morning, again mom woke up late. Dad helped in making Idlies and chutney. I am sick of this food, especially when dad prepares it. It doesn't have the same softness as prepared by mom. Requested mom to prepare Dosa, she politely tried to convince me.

Only fifteen minutes for school's first bell. Already we went late one-day last week. If we go late today, we will get fine. If a teacher receives a late fine, it spreads like wildfire. Mom putting maximum effort to avoid that.

She put four Idlies on the plate and pleaded me to eat it. Ignored and yelled for Dosa. Right at the moment, dad asked to get him his file or something. Furious mom went near the room and shouted. Had never seen mom in real anger and yelling before.

She came out and searched for something. Sure, it is not for dad's, something she lost it seems. Dad hugged mom and whispered something in her ear. He came close to me and suggested to quietly eat the food. I strongly opposed and yelled '*I want Dosa, only Dosa!*'

Dad murmured, 'You don't want to be stubborn today. Your mom is furious. Take my advice, eat whatever you have.' I shook my head fiercely. Dad patted on my shoulder and left.

It seems mom had finally found the missing object. She quickly went to the kitchen, grabbed a plate, and begin to eat. She stood still in shock to see me sitting hands folded and angrily staring at my plate.

She ran towards me and screamed, 'Why haven't you had your breakfast? Come on, eat fast.' Looked at her in sheer anger, 'I want Dosa, nothing else. Will not eat this.' Forcefully pushed the plate away.

Mom in a firm tone, 'Listen...' I closed my ears by my hands and shouted, 'Dosa... Dosa...' Didn't allow her to talk at all. Her face turned cruel, 'Final warning...' again chanted for Dosa and didn't let her speak.

A fierce slap on my right cheek. The force at which I got that hit, almost all my teeth came out. Bell rang on my ears and kept on ringing. Slowly lowered my hands, tears on my eyes because of the pain that I am enduring on my cheek and in my heart. Flipped my lips and ready to cry.

Mom yelled like a loudspeaker, 'Silently finish the breakfast before I finish, else you will get more slaps.' Scared to death, didn't say a single word, no tears grabbed the plate immediately and quickly begin to eat without seeing mom's cruel face.

After breakfast, mom forcefully tied my shoelace, and I didn't get her usual hug and kiss before leaving to my class.

This can't be my mom. She yelled at me. All I asked for was a Dosa, and she beat me for it?

She became like these cruel, strict, heartless teachers, who enjoy hurting little kids. I never understood when my friends talk about their mom beating. Always thought that they are not their actual mom. Today realised I am totally wrong.

Will I get more slaps? Is every day going to be like this? Mom has become this cruel person that I am afraid of. She hates me, And I hate her very much.

The impression of her fingers was on my cheek for almost the whole first period of school. Can't bear the pain of that slap from mom. Not on the face, but deep into my heart and brain, where it hurts the most.

Chapter – 6: Hardest Thing

Leaning on those broad shoulders of Akash, makes me forget all the troubles, shred sorrows and always brings positive energy. Today I need the most.

Akash wiping my tears, 'Stop crying, darling! You are making me feel highly uncomfortable. Please...'

I hid my face on his shoulder, 'I beat him, Akash. Slapped so hard that the impression of fingers lasted for an hour.'

Akash softly moved his fingers over my face and made me look into his eyes. 'Krish should know he can't be stubborn about certain things. His skin is so soft and white, even when I lift him for a few seconds, his skin turns a dark reddish colour. Don't worry, he is fine. You spoke with him at lunch and spent time on his regular homework. For what you are crying? I don't understand.'

Embraced him softly and said, 'He is not speaking in the same manner. He is acting differently. Besides, this is the first time he persisted on seeking something. Not even once he hadn't listened to me. All he asked is for a Dosa. Could have spared five more minutes for him.'

Akash pecked on my cheek, 'This is exactly what we discussed. This is how it starts. He just asked this and that. You will try to figure out a way to fulfil everything he is seeking. He will never have self-esteem or pride and will never be able to figure out right or wrong. Every parent raising a child should hold the responsibility of bringing their kid a good human being. The more you try to do everything for him, he will lose the will to act on his own.'

Patted lightly on his shoulder, 'Why you have to make such a big deal out of small, small things? He is not like any other kids; he listens to everything and never does any mischiefs.'

Akash smiled mildly, 'That's also a problem. You have cuddled him so deep into your world. For him you are everything, and you are his world. He never looks outside. Tell me how much time you stayed at home after school when you are his age?'

I had a naive expression. Akash continued, 'I thought so. He doesn't even go outside reasoning to do homework with you. Do you think he can't solve three-digit multiplication problems on his own?'

'He can solve four-digits multiplication problems. Math comes much easier for him than me.' I responded proudly, bragging about my son, failing to read the context of Akash's point of view.

Akash applauded, 'Great! Yet, for these silly things, every day he sits with you and you unnecessarily waste time. You are not letting him grow up. Remember when mom has to pitch-in and tell you to reduce breastfeeding slowly as Krish was growing up? You never give thought on these things, always needs someone to remind.'

My face became dull and after few seconds broke the silence, 'Still... shouldn't have to slap him.' Akash gave a deep breath, 'When mom died, the first few days were difficult for me. I couldn't manage work, you and Krish. Left home mostly in frustration. Soon realised I am not properly handling things and slowly figured out ways to remain calm, reduce my anger and manage everything. You are just at the same space right now; I am sure you will find a way soon. Don't worry about it, take it easy.'

Again, in a deep sorrow tone, 'I don't want to punish Krish for my inability to handle the situation.' Akash like a feather rolled his fingers on my cheek, and I rested my face on his huge palm. 'Dear, you must move on and stop blaming yourself for everything. He acted stubbornly and persisted. You made him realise it won't work like that. There is nothing wrong here.'

Closed my eyes and said, 'Had agreed to you on everything, Akash. Joined the school, reduced spending time with him, by taking needless notes of a lesson for students with pictures and made him eat by himself. Feel we are throwing suddenly too many surprises for Krish. Shall we postpone going to my cousin's home?'

Tightly cuddled Akash. He politely replied, 'We discussed this, Hema. We are not doing anything suddenly. Taking things as planned, step-by-step. He needs to learn how to handle himself without us around him, socialise with people, accept differences, and mingle.

You can't be there always to tie his shoes, cross the roads, help his homework and many things which he must do by himself. For me, he is already too old and too smart for a few things.'

'He will learn, and he is a fast learner. Just worried that we might lose him trying to force the issue. He is just a little boy.' Murmured.

Akash patting me slowly, 'Yes, He is little, and he won't understand immediately. Eventually, he will. Guarantee you, we will not lose our son. He will become a better person when we come back, have my word on it.'

Though Akash assurance gave me a little relief, not that confident as him. For me, his views and words are golden standard and never ever looked the other way around. He understood my loneliness, and he purely wants me to be happy.

While the thoughts are going on my mind, Akash chuckled, 'You know, Krish calls Suji "*Evil Demon Witch*" Mainly because she teases him.'

Hugged him tightly, 'Hopefully, his point of view changes when we return. Had asked Suji to a little bit lenient on Krish.'

Akash responded, 'She can't change much. Our son must not get frustrated by her and give it back smartly. Krish must understand each person is different and just because they do things he doesn't like doesn't mean they are evil. He must see the goodness in Suji, learn to see good in people irrespective who they are.'

'A massive ask from a little boy.' Replied retaking my son's side. Know Akash is right and he is trying to make our son better person with empathy and more like him.

The plan to leave for cousin home next week remained confidential between my parents and me. They are very eager to spend some alone time with their grandson. They have been telling me to visit cousin Meera's new-born baby girl for more than six months. Finally, we scheduled for next weekend.

Krish doesn't know about it. He always comes with us where ever we go. This time, Akash is travelling for an official meeting that happens on Saturday in the nearby city of my cousin's residential place, and I am just tagging along with Akash. It's a deliberate attempt to leave Krish with someone else apart from Akash and me. Praying for everything to go smooth.

Chapter – 7: Loneliness

Hardly able to concentrate at my class after that thunderous slap from mom. At lunchtime, mom spoke softly, but the fear is rooted in my heart, hesitantly spoke with her.

At home, she is deliberately skipping our playing time. Also, scared of getting thrashes, kept a little distance. To my relief, next week, grandpa and grandma came. Thoroughly enjoyed the evening, playing hide and seek, catch, and catch and many other games.

Had little idea that they are here to take care of me on mom's absence. Mom and dad had never left me alone. Even when grandpa got sick, dad stayed with me, only mom went to see him, that too for just one day. Now, for three days, I must be alone with my grandparents and the devil.

Sure, the devil will torture me to the extreme. Pleaded mom and dad to take me with them. Dad cunningly had my grandparents nearby whenever I plea and cornered me to accept their stay. Without a choice had to stay alone.

Till Friday lunchtime, mom was with me. When we are alone having lunch, I asked her the most critical question that I wanted to ask her for a while, 'Are you leaving me because you became a teacher? Would you have left me alone when you are only my mom?'

Mom tried to convince me giving several explanations. Felt all her reasons are invalid. She twice or thrice suggested me to play in the ground with my friends and Suji. Playing with my friends is fine, what's this playing with the devil? Starting to hate my mom as equally as my aunt. In fact, both sisters are the same, cruel persons.

Friday evening, the devil came to pick me from the school. Unlike other times at home, she smiled bizarrely. Was about to vomit after seeing that horrible smile. As usual, she kissed, making my cheek completely wet.

She was extra cautious in crossing the road and held my hands tightly. I wasn't in any mood to do homework and hence struggled a lot. Surprisingly, the devil helped me. The evil demon, read my whole lesson, prepared something, and explained me in a much simpler and easy way as mom does.

The way that demon spoke was nothing like her usual inscrutable slang. She spoke clearly in the way I can understand. I think the devil speaks weirdly only because of that lipstick and painting on the face. Today, no painting, no lipstick and spoke politely. Even when I made mistakes, she corrected me and gave suggestions to rectify my mistakes.

Seriously, this can't be the same demon. The first time, felt a very tiny bit bad for considering her as an evil demon. Deserves to be called as "*Suji aunty*" Can clearly see mom had trained her. Still blamed mom for not teaching her how to hug gently and kiss delicately.

The dinner was the worst I had in recent times. Nothing like how mom does. My aunt tried to force me to eat initially, later let me go. She thoughtfully cut a whole apple for me. Mom always gives fruits once in a day, so had no problem in having that.

Next day morning, during breakfast, grandma kept on asking to have one more Dosa and tell me when my stomach is full. Till date, rarely knew the quantity I ate, as always mom knows how much I need to eat and gives accordingly. I drank two tumblers of water and felt stomach full.

At the playground, joined with my friends and played cricket for a while. Unable to digest the cheating some of them do. It was not really fun. Few times fight broke out. Dad always tells stories of his playing days; seems he lived on a different planet where every kid played the game by rules. Felt hunger after playing a couple of games. It was a bad idea to drink too much water.

Back at home, Suji aunty was preparing lunch. Since, had nothing else to do, sat near her and grandma. The dish made by Suji aunty was awful. Wanted to spit it out; couldn't, because of my aunt's face. She had put a lot of effort into making this dish, and she is eagerly waiting for me to eat the whole and praise her.

Struggled to swallow and ate half plate only for my aunt. She did turn from evil to angel just for me.

Evening, we went outside, and all three kept on asking what do I want? Haven't asked for anything before. Mom buys me everything, and sometimes dad does. Never really had to ask for anything.

Grandma and grandpa praised me so much for being such a nice boy. Didn't understand what special had I done? Started to wonder whether they really know about kids. They are acting cluelessly as if I am the first kid they know.

Sunday morning, Suji aunty went for some course. Decided to stay at home because of yesterday's bad experience on the playground. Played with grandpa for some time. He started to breathe heavily and cough severely.

Nobody to play, nothing to do, felt completely alone. Never felt so boring in my life.

Lost patience and went back to the ground to play with my friends. Understood, how things are going to pan out, so decided not to get into fights. Cheating is wrong and felt very bad when others did. But I played by the rules as mom told. Suggested to my friends to correct it, when they broke a rule, but never got into an argument.

When I came back for lunch, the old devil was back. Full of painting on the face, light red colour lipstick, long earrings, worse dress and of course, she teased me.

In the evening, the same Suji aunty behaved softly. She definitely has some problem. I think it's because of overheat outside. Thought of the way I handled my friends today. Implied the same logic when aunty teased me at dinner and instead of anger, we enjoyed running around and playing.

Finally, I taught Suji aunty how to kiss delicately without watering the other person's cheek. She is a quick learner like me and took my advice immediately.

Thought these two days are going to be terrible, not so much. Felt occasional loneliness and boredom, but importantly found my aunty is not an evil demon.

Chapter – 8: Good and Bad

The first time my little honey is staying away from me for this long. Trying to smile and appear happy, couldn't fake it properly all the time.

Cannot pass by a minute without thinking about Krish. He didn't speak properly when I called him, clearly showing his displeasure. It was an expected reaction from him, yet it hurts.

Gave few tips to Meera on raising the child. Things I learnt from my mom and mother-in-law. She might have had more such advice from many people. So, kept them to the limit, considering not to confuse her.

Akash tried to deviate my thoughts to something else, other than worrying about Krish. He failed immensely. Even on the whole journey back home, kept on talking about Krish. Don't know how Akash listens to everything patiently. It's crystal clear from where Krish gets patience and tolerance.

My little sweetheart was in deep sleep when we reached home. I couldn't get much sleep. Woke up very early in the morning and sat next to cutely sleeping Krish.

Hard to explain his sleeping position. He had pushed the pillow, and head rested on his hands, turned to his right and legs stretched across. With all the weird positions, a mild smile on his lips. Akash tells it's not possible for any six-year-old kid to smile in sleep and I am just assuming too many things. Well, he is still only a dad, couldn't understand this.

Most of the time, I read Krish's through his expressions on sleep. His cute tremendously mild smile brought me plenty of happiness. But it didn't last for long. He was all alone without me, and he is happy? A slight niggle. Possessiveness and jealousy made me feel insecure for a moment.

Keenly waited for my sweetheart to wake up from the bed. Krish's hug felt more like a formality, couldn't feel the usual love. Consoled and prepared to see the change in him, especially with Suji.

Unlike earlier, he enjoyed teasing Suji, and they were having fun. What we hoped for, happened. He became more attached to my mom and dad too.

One hand the happiness was exceeding, on the other, felt terrible when Krish gave more importance to his grandparents than me. He had pushed me to the second position.

The hugs, kisses and cute expressions were missing. Initially, cried on Akash's shoulder whenever Krish avoided me and provide more importance to others. Slowly adjusting to reality.

Every day might have heard a hundred times, the word, "*mom*" now couldn't hear once a day. Difficult to ignore my instinct, possessiveness, and smile, when he says he loves his grandparents more than his actual parents.

Akash gave me the strength to cope with all this. Can see Krish is doing things intentionally to hurt me. Akash talked me out to see the goodness in that. He claims Krish is also way too possessive and couldn't handle me giving priority to other stuff. Akash persists Krish will understand soon. Hopefully, he is right.

Going to school, living my passion, sounded wonderful. The cost of that selfish happiness was way too much. Everyday things getting only worse between my sweetheart and me. I couldn't find a single good thing that happened out of this for me on this.

The weekends were even longer as Krish spend most of the time at the playground. Akash tried to evict my loneliness. In the process, I am having fun, teasing, doing pranks, as we get more alone time now. Akash desperately trying to keep me happy, performing all tricks in his book.

At school, slowly started to become friendlier with the kids. Can sense strong bonding and few parents appreciated my work personally.

For the first time in a very long time, felt I had achieved something significant. When little kids consider you as a friend, teaching them becomes extremely easy. The key factors were tolerating their little mistakes, correcting, and making them better.

Because of the derived happiness, perfectly managing work and life. No rush getting ready to school, no yelling or anger. Only smile and happiness.

The only niggle is my son's distance from me. Know I haven't lost him completely. Hoping he would understand and I will be back to the first position in his heart.

The quarterly examination results came, and my class secured hundred percentage pass record. The praises came from every part of the school, including the parents. Always dreamt of such a day in my life.

Received an award during the prayer session for my performance as a teacher and the way of my teaching, with huge rounds of applauds. Akash was there to see me receive the award as I dearly wanted him to view it.

After a very happy week, the new morning started uncomfortably. Something in my instinct is telling me something wrong about to happen. Couldn't exactly guess.

The creepy feeling grew more prominent in the class, making me unable to concentrate fully on the class. Thunder and lightning made children shiver, controlling them took a lot out of me.

Steady rain falling outside brought more thunders to my heart, beating faster than a bullet train. Closed my eyes and prayed to all the Gods.

About lunchtime, school's clerk came running towards my class. My heart beat raised further. She folded the umbrella and came inside the class, 'Hema, mam, Krish got injured while playing on the PT hour. Nothing to worry, only a scratch. He is at first-aid bay near the Central Stage.'

Derived by an unnecessary guilty feel, thanked the clerk for the information and requested to look over the class, while I go and visit Krish.

Chapter – 9: No Substitute

Seeing mom right at the start of Monday morning, brought me a lot of happiness. But she left me alone intentionally. The mood swung from delightfulness to sorrow in a matter of seconds and ended by a hug, hesitantly.

More kisses for grandparents and Suji aunty. At school, heard a couple of my friends talking about making feel others jealous. Though not wholly aware of the process, more or less, got the idea.

From next day onwards, praised my grandma whenever I got the opportunity. Also, became close to my sweet aunty. My friends' circle grew every day and spent very little time with my mom.

Mom twice or thrice pleaded, almost begged to play with her. Villain dad stopped that and yelled at me for acting weird. I didn't want to argue with Villain and remembered the slap given by my heartless mom.

Next day at school, mom didn't come to our usual place for lunch. Lost my patience after a few minutes, went towards her class. It was incredibly horrible and heart-breaking to watch.

Little kids were hugging and kissing my mom... no. Not my mom. Mrs Hema Akash. She was happily laughing and lifting them. One or two kids even called her *"mom"* I assumed, them calling her mom will make her angry. Instead, she kissed on the kid's cheek. Mrs Hema Akash had become a mother of forty more children.

The love and care available only for me are now available for forty more. They are more important for her than me. She ignores me for them. Is she taking revenge on me?

Tears poured out of my eyes, unable to hide my sadness, rushed towards restroom and washed my face again and again. Had one of the saddest lunches at school.

After deep thought, decided to cut my dependency on Mrs Hema Akash. Prepared a list of items on which I depend on her. The list went more than one page and made me angrier.

Created a list with top ten items and the first thing is tying my shoelace. Kept on torturing dad to teach me. Dad spent more than two hours to teach me. He has more patience than I thought. Well, not to the level of Mrs Akash, but he does have some.

Though I didn't want to call her mom, the things on my list are getting highly impossible by each passing day. Cooking food is the most difficult. The best cook is Mrs Akash, everybody else is a distant second. She is the best in everything.

To my irritation, more kids hugged and kissed her. Everyone praised her and identified me as Mrs Hema's son. I would have been very proud of that a few months ago. Now, getting a mixed feeling.

Then, my friends started to praise her and told I am the luckiest boy to have such a mom. Many said I am gifted. The principal gave an award for mom where the whole school clapped. They gave a speech praising her and about all her greatness.

Of course, she is great, and everyone's fav. But, that's my problem. Everything was only for me, and she was entirely mine.

She was only my mom. Now, she is sweeter to other children, care, and love, whereas I became nothing to her.

My hate on her grew. She is not worried much about me. One day I even saw her playing catch, and catch with dad. I can clearly understand her priorities now.

Dad is not a villain anymore and became more like a friend. He is good. At least, he remains constant, doesn't change like mom.

Thunder and lightning followed by heavy rain. We are not inside the classroom. At the playground, enjoying the wetness and rain. Jumping, running, catching, and laughing. The PT master tried his level best to get us back to the classroom before the heavy rain. The classroom is a long way, and we decided to enjoy on the road.

While running, one boy tripped off a stone and fell on me. Unable to keep the balance, I too fall and skate for some distance. A big wound on my knees, difficult to walk, blood pouring out. Screamed for mom.

The doctor at school was ready to inject me with a huge syringe. Mom came worried running towards me. I jumped and hugged her, forgetting all the hate. After a very long time without any hesitancy.

She convinced the doctor not to inject. She argued and fought for me. She understands my pain. My old mom who genuinely cares about me is back. She hasn't changed entirely yet.

We went early to home and dad arrived soon. Dad was furious on mom and scolded her for not injecting me.

I tried to intervene, only provoked him to grab me and take to the doctor. Mom didn't try to stop. Dad accepted doctor's suggestion to inject me. The big needle went deep inside. The pain was thrice than that of my fall.

I was barely able to sit because of the injection. Dad or anybody there didn't understand my pain. Sure, mom would have known.

Back at home to mom, only she bothered about my pain. She would have talked anyone out, except for dad.

The whole night spent hugging mom. Next day, dad accepted for me to remain at home. Mom and dad left, as usual, leaving my aunt to stay with me. I had no problem hanging out with Suji aunty.

Next day morning, unusually felt severe body pain. Unable to even move. I can hear mom whispering, but couldn't answer her.

Mom never left my side for the next two days. I can see her crying occasionally.

Had I got it wrong? If I am not important to her, why she didn't go to school? Filled in thoughts, hugged mom tightly. Next day, pain has gone and briskly played hide and seek with mom. Same smile, same love, same hugs, and kisses.

Monday, went to school and heard more praises for mom. Few teachers praised me for being such a good boy and conveyed my mom has brought me well.

Their statement made me think from a different angle. Stood across differently angles inside my classroom during lunchtime to get various angles.

Chapter – 10: Being Special

The screams of Krish when the doctor took the injection, shuddered me. I know TT injection is vital to prevent serious infections. Yet, the tears of Krish made me weak again. Unable to bear, convinced the doctor to not inject.

At home, Akash scolded me severely for skipping TT injection. He yelled at me and explained the possibility of infections and took Krish forcefully to the doctor.

A crying Krish hugged me tightly. I can't control myself from crying. Though I couldn't have done anything to prevent Krish's injury, felt guilty for not taking care of my son properly.

Akash suggested Krish to take leave for a couple of days. I too agreed on the same and went to the school as usual. Unexpectedly, the next day morning, Krish body was burning at very high temperature.

The doctor assured it is only seasonal fever and nothing to worry. Felt guiltier of not staying and taking care of Krish. Akash tried to convince me that none of this is my fault, failed in his attempt.

Maybe Krish is right. Considering my happiness over his, selfishly acted, not as a mother. Akash was utterly against the idea I am getting into and desperately trying to persuade me to think of something else.

Krish health improved quickly, and in a day, he began to walk, run, and play. After a very long time, got the opportunity to play with my sweetheart. In a few days as usual got ready for school.

I spoke with Akash on quitting the job and staying at home, taking care of Krish. Akash was completely against it. He told me that I will spoil Krish's social progress and hinder his development.

In a mixed state of mind, wondering what's the right choice, decided to think clearly, take time, and conclude on what to do next.

*** *** ****

The different angles helped me again. Mom was always there for me, even though I tried to avoid her. She still takes care of me every day from morning to evening.

I can't even cross the main road without her. Tying shoelace is the only thing that I am able to manage myself. Everything else is still the same.

Was very proud of my ability to speak and write English. Proud of my high 90+ marks. Everything I achieved so far is because of her. She taught me everything. Everyone praises my character and behaviour because I follow whatever my mom has taught me.

One problem though is that she is now mom for forty other children, not a teacher. She was never cruel or strict. She slapped because I didn't obey and troubled her. Anybody else would have done the same. Even had I listened to my dad, might have escaped from that hit.

Dad always advises having *"empathy"* Never really understood the meaning of the word. Today is the day to realise. Thinking from other's position.

Now, the first question, why she decided to become a teacher? Because she felt boring at home when dad had left for the office, and I went to school. One hour, just one hour, when Suji aunty was not there to play, I couldn't bear the boredom and went to play in a place that I hate completely. How mom might have felt when she was all alone for so many days?

Is everything my fault? I am the reason for my own suffering? Was this advice to think from mom's point of view was dad trying to say all these times? Oh... no... what have I done? How mom felt when I intentionally avoided her? I am the most special and important person for her, and I hurt her?

When someone praises mom, always felt very proud. But now, I feel terrible for that? It's not a correct thing.

Started to feel ashamed of me. Should have listened to the villain on the first Saturday after mom became a teacher. Ok, ask sorry, console mom, and get back as before.

Mom was preparing dinner, and Suji aunty was inside in her room, studying. Anxiously waiting for some alone time with mom. I believe I showed my restlessness quite openly for dad to notice.

Dad closed his laptop and curiously, 'Is there something you want?' Turned towards him, thought for a moment, stared towards the kitchen, and decided to sit and discuss with dad.

Slowly walked and sat next to dad, 'Realised there are both good and bad in mom becoming a teacher for me. Going to ask sorry.'

Dad curious face became happy, 'Good! Anyone influenced you to have this thinking?' I kept a straight face, 'Maybe you and mom? Based on both of your advice, thought from different angles, and understood my mom is still the same and only she had become a teacher to help more kids like me.'

Dad gave a pause and asked, 'Because you got sick and mom took care, don't...' I interrupted before dad finish with a mild smile, 'No... saw from her point of view, like you said with the word.... What's that? Empathy! Plus, I learned everything from her. She taught me how to speak, write, walk, run and everything.

Her love for me will never reduce. She can't bear my pain then, now, and always. Like my friends say I am the luckiest boy to have such a mom. I am proud of my mom when little kids younger than me call her as "*mother*" instead of a teacher. My mom is always special, and everyone loves her. Nobody can hate her.'

Dad patted on my shoulder, 'Wow! That was some talk for a six-year-old kid. Your mom taught you well on storytelling. I am proud of you too for thinking like this at such a young age.'

The smile widened on my face, 'That's what you both wanted, right? For me to grow up, understand better and mature faster than you guys did?' On answering took a dig at dad.

Dad chortled, 'Very clever and sarcastic. You know, I am the reason for all these. I convinced, no... forced your mom to go to school as a teacher, reduce helping you in doing your homework, leaving you alone with Suji and your grandparents.

I wanted you to handle and look after yourself. You shouldn't be dependent on us forever. Slowly, you should learn to do your own thing by yourself.

Socialising and adjusting are very important in any environment. You won't learn that by having your home and family as your entire world. You must go out, explore, and face unfair situations. I am sure these last few months taught you a lot.'

My smile reduced and furiously stared at dad, 'I always knew you were the villain.' Dad chortled again, 'And thinking from various angles mean having different perceptions, views and thoughts. Not walking across the room at different angles.'

In an aggressive tone, 'Had found that after the first-day mom became teacher itself. Yet, walking across makes me think better. Hence, I do that.' After a few seconds, we both laughed.

Suji aunty came from the room running towards me to grab and shake me. I quickly moved away. She screamed, 'I am more beautiful than your mom!' Mom came out of the kitchen, and I know Suji aunty spoiled my plans. Still, the demons exist. Somehow need to turn it around.

'My mom won't paint her face like you. She is naturally beautiful than you!' I moved away from Suji aunty towards mom. Suji aunty in a weird slang, 'blah... blah... Only confident people dress like me. Your...'

Didn't want to allow her to keep on bragging, 'Everyone will like you for your character and behaviour. One day, when you have a son, he won't look for this cheap painting and colouring. He will love you the same irrespective of how your face looks. Learn some good characters from my mom. So that, your son can be as proud as I am and say that *"my mom is the best"*' Immediately went near mom. Stolen that line partially from two sentimental movies that I saw recently.

I can see tears in my mom's eyes about to fall. She bent towards me and lifted. I hugged her tightly, 'Sorry mom! You are my mom, and you are always very special to me. Thank you for being there, then, now, and always!' Kissed her delicately with full of love and joy.

'And I am very proud of you. You are the best teacher in the world. Your students don't call you "*teacher*" they call you "*mom*" Every kid likes you so much and I will always proudly say "*My mom is the best in the whole world!*"

Mom hugged tightly, kissed on both my cheeks and on the forehead, 'You are my golden sweetheart! Ohh... dear!' Suji aunty wanted to tease back, but gave our moment and slowly went away and sat on the sofa next to dad.

*** *** ****

Akash persistence making me more confused. He reluctantly reminds me of doing what I love, and my happiness is the key to the entire family's happiness.

In mixed feeling, was preparing dinner, interrupted by Suji's loud voice. Switched off the stove and kept the vessel to cool. With a kind smile on my face, went towards the hall.

Suji's usual remarks. The follow-up answer of Krish was something extremely filmy but made me very happy. Krish took a stand for me after a long time. He thrashed Suji by his response. This quick turnaround is what I expected.

Always dreamt of hearing something like this from Krish. From what he said and the way he said, I clearly understood he is considering me back as his mom, as before.

Though the dialogue seems filmy, it brought tears in my eyes. Waiting for Krish to move towards me. The feel when your son says he is proud of you... only parents can feel and describe.

The jump and hug filled with full of unconditional love. A sweet little peck on your cheek; the most satisfying, joyful, and complete feeling for a mom. I don't want anything more. I got my son back. He is mine, and I raised above everyone else in his heart.

Tightly hugged and kissed him in extreme happiness. With tears and smile, a satisfaction of a complete family, slowly turned towards Akash who is smiling and looking at me pleasantly.

Appendices

Main Characters
Krish
Hema – Krish's Mom
Akash – Krish's Dad
Sujitha – Hema's Sister

Glossary

HM – Headmaster

KG – Kinder Garten

PF – Pension Fund

PT – Physical Training

TT – Tetanus Toxoid

Inspirations

Still remember the day, when my mom decided to become a teacher at my school, I was a little kid studying in KG class. Felt highly uncomfortable on hearing this news. Though I don't remember how things proceeded further, I remember the feeling of lost on that day.

This incident was the inspiration for me to write this story. This book is not based on a real-life event or fact; instead, a fiction work scripted over an incident that I vaguely remember, enhanced with numerous sensitive human emotions dramatically.

To the Readers

My works are proofread and edited only by me. I don't come from a literary background and have a limited vocabulary, just like writing. Hence, there may be a possibility of spelling, grammatical and punctuation mistakes. I sincerely apologise for the errors and assure you that I will keep on learning and improving myself to prevent these mistakes and increase my vocabulary. Thanks for the consideration.

I believe that the most precious thing in this world should be something that's impossible to get back. Everything in the world has a cost and bought in some way, by money or gold or actions or speech. The one thing that doesn't have a quantitative value and impossible to buy back by anyone in this world is "*Time*."

Thank you very much for spending your precious time reading my writing.

Have a pleasant rest of the day!

Also by P G Seshagopal

My Bad Friend
Is It There?
Not My Mom Anymore
A Brief Look into Freshers' IT Job Interviews